Sparks Fly

"I want to offer you a proposal."

Brenda cocked her head to the side and looked at Marcus. She had a feeling what it would be about, but she wasn't 100 percent sure.

"What proposal is that, Marcus?"

"I'm just going to say it. I am attracted to you, Brenda, and I want to do things to your body like I have to no other."

Brenda couldn't believe the words coming out of his mouth. Could this be happening to her? Could this be true? Brenda wanted the same thing. She couldn't even speak; she just nodded her head.

"Follow me into the bathroom, Brenda. I want to do things to your body that cannot wait until we land. If you are interested, meet me in the bathroom in two minutes."

Marcus got up and walked away.

An Imprint of Jasmine Barton-Moore Publishing House
Copyright © 2017 Jasmine Barton-Moore
All rights reserved.

ISBN number 978-0-9991789-0-4 Paperback
ISBN number 978-0-9991789-1-1 ebook
www.jasminebartonmoorepublishinghouse.com

Sparks Fly

JASMINE BARTON-MOORE

Dear reader,

I am happy to present to you my first book. When I first started writing this book, I thought to myself, who would really enjoy reading what I had to say on paper? Who would want to read my work? But there was this burning sensation that I just needed to write. I could create amazing stories. I decided, why not become an author?

My style of writing is still a little fresh, but I am learning as I go along. I know when it comes to writing, there is a rule, but I wanted to write the way people would understand me.

I followed my heart and went for it. Dreams really do come true; you just have to make them happen, work hard, and believe in yourself. I am so thankful for all the support from friends and family and being surrounded by positivity.

I can do all things through Christ which strengtheneth me.
—Philippians 4:13

To my love,

I would like to dedicate this book to my mom, may her soul rest in peace. My mom was always there to encourage me to push myself in life, and she reminded me to never settle for less. Even though she had her own demons to fight with, my mom was always there no matter what. We only get one life, and I plan on living this life to the fullest.

CHAPTER ONE

BRENDA TURNER TRIED to live a simple life—
except for the messy divorce she had just gone
through with her cheating ex-husband. And now
that her life was finally settling back down, she got news
that her ex-husband had been murdered, and there were no
suspects. They just found his blood all over his apartment
and assumed that there were no survivors. Brenda wasn't
surprised before she found out he was cheating on her, he
had suspicious ways. Come to find out he was up to his
neck in gambling and owed a lot of money to loan sharks.
Somedays he even looked lost. She remembered asking him
if everything was OK and he flipped out on her.

She didn't know what he had gotten himself into, but
she was just glad he was out of her life. At first she was bitter
about the divorce because they had only been married a
little under a year. She had met him around the time she
lost her mother. In the beginning he always did sweet things
for her. The crazy thing was, he had begged her not to get
the divorce, but she didn't want to be with a cheater because

there was no telling how long he had been doing it for. That was over a year and a half ago.

Sometimes she wished she had her mom here to have someone to talk to, but a year ago her mom had been in a head-on collision with a drunk driver, causing her instant death. The driver sped off from the scene of the crash but was found hours later, just a few miles down the road in a ditch. That's why it had taken so long for him to be found. After the head-on collision, the drunk driver had run into a tree and died instantly. So no one would be held accountable for her mother's death.

It had always been just Brenda and her mom. She never knew about her father and anytime she would bring it up her mom would change the subject, so Brenda stopped asking. Now more than anything, she felt alone in the world. Her mom was her rock. Brenda's mom had always told her she could do anything in this world that she wanted to do; all she had to do was put her mind to it, and it would get done.

Brenda felt the tears burning the back of her eyes. So she began thinking happy thoughts.

Brenda had to get out of her funk. Tonight she was off on a vacation to Italy for four weeks. As she triple-checked her bags, Brenda was thankful that she could work from home because it gave her the leisure to travel when and wherever she wanted.

Brenda thought back to the times when she had worked at jobs that she had absolutely hated. She had worked at a highly demanding law firm for a few years before she decided that was not the life she wanted to live. All the endless nights and no time to herself—that's when she'd decided enough was enough.

But no matter what, she always thought back to her mom, and her mom was always there in spirit to encourage her to do what she loved most. That was to write novels.

Now that she was sure she had everything for her trip, Brenda sat her belongings by the door and looked herself over again in the mirror. She decided to keep it casual by wearing jeans, a white V-neck, a baseball cap, and her Chucks. She wanted to be as comfortable as possible, considering that her flight from Chicago to Italy would be ten hours long.

Brenda was born in DC, but after she had married, she moved to Chicago. And even after the divorce, she still decided to stay there. There was something about Chicago that she loved and didn't want to leave. But she was happy to be off to paradise tonight.

As she heard the taxi's horn, she grabbed her bags and stepped outside. It was a cold, windy October day in Chicago. This was one of her favorite seasons, when the leaves changed colors. She loved the feeling of the wind blowing in her hair. Even though she loved this type of weather, she did make sure to bundle up. Brenda got in her taxi and rode to the airport. The traffic was light, so it only took about twenty minutes to get to the airport.

Brenda looked around the airport and was surprised by how packed it was for an evening flight and it was a Wednesday. She was the type of woman who didn't care about hat hair. She loved to keep her look simple. She was able to find a seat next to an older woman near her gate in which she would departure from.

Brenda felt the heating in the airport to be unbearable, so she removed her hat and coat leaving her hair still in a ponytail. She took out her iPad, her headphones, and her sandwich, which she had packed as a snack. She had a good three hours before her flight's departure, so she made herself comfortable.

That was the only thing Brenda hated about flying especially internationally: you needed to be at the airport hours before your flight just in case there were any delays with your travels. And it was just her luck that everything with her flight was running smoothly, so she had nothing but time to kill.

Marcus King stood near the departure gate where he knew his plane would be taking off. He glanced down at a picture of a woman named Brenda, his next assignment. She looked like the average woman, not really someone he would be interested in.

One of his longtime friends, Kennedy Jackson, had asked him for a favor. Marcus looked up to Kennedy like a father figure, since his dad had walked out of his life when he was only five. His father never gave an explanation as to why he was leaving. Marcus thought that he probably couldn't take the pressure of being a father and was overwhelmed, so he decided to leave.

Marcus felt that he owed his friend this favor because when Marcus and his twin brother, CJ, got into trouble, Kennedy had been the one to bail them out. Kennedy had just showed up out of nowhere and decided to help. He was a lawyer just passing through.

Marcus thought back to those times. Him and his brother were boosting high-end cars and would resell them on the black market. But of course all good things must come to an end, and they got caught.

Now that Marcus was older, he knew why he had done the things he had did. His mother had been a single parent and barely making ends meet, so he and his brother wanted to pull their weight. Just by Kennedy stepping in when he did he was able to lessen their sentence to only house arrest. Marcus had asked Kennedy why he had helped them out when they were nothing but strangers to him.

Kennedy had said, "I can see the good in both you and your brother, and everyone deserves a second chance."

Kennedy had asked them what they wanted to do in life, and he gave them the money to start their private-investigating company. And even though Marcus had paid his debt in full, he still felt that if it wasn't for this man, he might not be where he is now.

When Kennedy had called and asked him and his

brother for a favor, he did not hesitate to help Kennedy. Marcus didn't ask his friend any questions; he just knew that Kennedy had sounded desperate on the phone, so he would get answers from him about the situation later. Plus, from the tone of Kennedy's voice, it sounded like he didn't want to go into detail, either.

All Marcus knew was that her name was Brenda Turner, that she was going on vacation to Italy for four weeks, and that she needed a bodyguard. It was a funny coincidence that they lived in the same state. Of course, with his job he had to know certain information about his clients. He knew everything there was to know about Brenda, even down to the kind of underwear she liked to wear.

As he looked around the airport just people watching, he found it amazing how much stuff people traveled with. He looked down at his watch and wondered when Brenda would show up. He glanced at the picture one more time, focusing on the shape of her face. She had a lovely smile.

That's when he felt an electrical shock pulse through his body, so he glanced up. It was as if time had stopped and he now only saw her in the airport. And there she was walking in. His heart began to beat a little faster, almost as if he had stopped breathing.

Her picture did her no justice. In person, her face was stunning; he could see her dimples in her cheeks, and he could see her bright hazel eyes from across the way. Her skin was smooth like caramel.

Her hair was in a small bun at the nape of her neck; just by looking at her bun he could tell she kept it in its natural state. The light in the airport made her honey-blond hair glow, but it was beautiful. Even though her hair was in a low ponytail he imagined running his fingers through her hair.

His eyes began to roam farther down. His eyes landed on her breasts for a moment or two. She was wearing a V-neck, so he got a great glimpse. She looked to be a C cup—nice, round, full breasts. She stood about five four and had long legs that went well with her curvy body.

Usually Marcus went for women who were at least five nine and slim, to go with his six-foot-three-inch frame, but with Brenda, height did not matter. He was too focused on how beautiful she was. She had a nice firm butt; you could tell she was the woman after his heart. Considering his heart was broken over a year ago when he found his ex-fiancé in bed with an old buddy of his.

She looked as if she worked out just enough to keep her frame intact. Or she just took really good care of her body. Most women whom Marcus dated made sure they had their makeup done and had the best clothes on; they always stepped outside looking as if they were about to be on the front cover of *Ebony* magazine. But not Brenda; she was dressed simply and comfortably. She was prepared for this flight to be a long one.

As he looked back up at her face, he caught her removing her hair tie. She began combing out her hair with her fingers. He choked a little a bit. Her hair looked even softer and bouncier than before. It complemented her skin. She looked as if she had been dipped into caramel; her skin was so silky smooth.

Everything about her screamed innocence. Now he had a million things running through his head, and the number one question was, why did she need a bodyguard?

Marcus watched as Brenda made her way to a free seat. He continued to look at her as she started pulling things out of her bag. He chuckled because she was one of those people who carried a lot of things around with her.

This is one of the reasons Marcus loved his job. He could study people. You could tell a lot about a person just by what they carried with them. He enjoyed bringing criminals to justice and getting people out of sticky situations, even the ones who needed protecting. He enjoyed not having to answer to anybody. He was still staring at her when the lady announced that their flight was boarding.

Brenda had just finished her sandwich when she looked up to see the stewardess announcing she could board the plane, that's when she found a tall, dark, and handsome man staring at her. He stood about six foot, and his body looked completely solid, as if he lived in the gym. He had dreads about waist length, which were pulled back into a ponytail. His skin was smooth like dark chocolate. His lips were a few shades lighter than his skin tone. His shoulders were broad, but a lean muscular body, with strong facial features. But he was one fine brother.

Brenda wasn't usually attracted to men with long hair; she always thought that it made them look a bit feminine. But not this man; everything about him screamed masculine and dangerous. He wore a black long-sleeve shirt, black pants, and black boots.

She didn't know how long he had been staring at her, but she knew he was checking her out. He had this hungry look in his eyes, like he wanted her. There was something about his eyes that did things to her body.

She looked deep into his dark, black eyes. It was hard for her to look away. It was as if they were the only two in the airport and he was undressing her with his eyes, and she stood there, just letting him. Brenda never would have just stood there, but she couldn't look away. She could see their bodies naked and pictured them touching each other all over.

She heard first class being called again. She hurriedly looked away from him, stood up, and walked in the direction of her plane since it was finally boarding time.

She gave the lady her ticket and was off, making an awkward moment not so awkward anymore. She hoped that he was not on the same plane as her. She didn't know what would happen if they were actually on the same plane, because nothing like that had ever happened to her before.

Brenda had chosen first class so that she could have the

extra space to stretch her legs out. She just hoped that she didn't sit next to a creepy person or somebody who wanted to talk to her. She wanted to get some work done.

Brenda saw herself as a nice person, but right now, she just wanted to be left alone so that she could enjoy the flight. She had made herself a promise not to work during her vacation. But she was on a plane, so she didn't count that. Brenda knew that sometimes she was a workaholic, but it got the bills paid and gave her the freedom to do what she liked.

She called her best friend, Jacki, to let her know she had made it on the plane safely. "Just letting you know I am waiting for my flight to take off."

Jacki said, "Girl, I am so excited you decided to take a trip; now close your computer and enjoy yourself. You might even meet some hot guy."

Brenda didn't dare tell her about what had just taken place in the airport. Brenda said, "How do you know my computer is open?"

"Because, Brenda, I know you and know how you operate."

Brenda just had to laugh. "Bye, girl."

"Bye, Brenda. Call me when you land."

"OK, I will," Brenda said and hung up the phone.

Jacki and Brenda had been good friends over the years, but they had become really close when Brenda went through that divorce with her ex-husband.

As she began to put in her earbuds, Brenda noticed those long, strong legs coming down the aisle toward her. She prayed that his seat would not be next to her seat. He stopped right in front of her row and put his bag in the overhead bin.

Brenda's eyes fell directly on his manhood, considering that it was at eye level. She couldn't believe that she was acting this way. She hurriedly looked away as he sat in the seat right next to hers. Brenda cursed herself inside her head.

Brenda was still staring at him. She was mesmerized by his beauty, so he said, "Hello."

Brenda had obviously been caught staring, so she hurried up and said, "Sorry," as she put the other earbud in.

CHAPTER TWO

MARCUS TOOK HIS seat next to Brenda; he had purposely gotten his seat next to her to get to know her better since she was the target and their flight would be ten hours.

That's where his team came along. That was another perk about his job he loved; he had a hacker by the name of Gary on his team who could hack into any system with his computer. Gary was the one who had coordinated their seats together.

Marcus knew he caught her off guard when he had caught her staring at him as he sat down. He looked over to her and saw that she was doing any- and everything not to make eye contact with him again. Her earbuds were in, and she was messing around with her laptop. But he could tell that she was still embarrassed. Her cheeks began to turn red; it was probably because she noticed him looking at her.

The flight attendant started talking about procedures of what to do if the plane was to lose control. Brenda could feel his eyes on her. She didn't know what was wrong with her; she just couldn't keep herself from smiling. It could be because she hadn't had sex in over a year. It could also be because there was a fine man staring at her. Brenda kept thinking maybe she should say something to him, but she didn't. She just sat there and pretended to be busy.

Marcus decided to put Brenda out of her misery and say something to her.

"So what are you listening to over there? By the way, I'm Marcus."

Brenda looked at the hand that was extended her way. She was considering if she should shake it or not, because if she did, that meant that they would probably talk for the whole flight, and did she want that? She could barely sit still with him just being next to her. But Brenda decided, what the hell. He was a handsome-looking black man.

She extended her hand and said, "Brenda, and I'm listening to classical music; it helps me relax, especially during a flight."

As soon as Brenda's hand went into his, Marcus felt that electrical shock that he had felt at the airport when he had noticed her walk into the room. It was as if everything stood still and he only saw Brenda on the plane.

His heart began to speed up, and his palms began to sweat. He removed his hand from hers. Marcus continued to stare at her and totally missed the question she just asked him.

"Hello, anybody in there?" she said.

Marcus heard her chuckle a little, and he liked the sound of her laugh. He could get used to that sound.

"Yeah, my bad. Now what were you asking me, Brenda?"

"I wanted to know, why are you going to Italy?"

Marcus smiled at her and said, "Business and maybe pleasure, too," meaning he wanted to get to know Brenda on a different level.

Brenda was a little disappointed; he seemed nice, but she didn't know about his playboy attitude. Even though she was on vacation to have fun, she was also a passionate person, and she didn't know if she just wanted a one-night stand.

She tossed the idea around in her head for a little while; she was on vacation, after all. Her friend, Jacki, had insisted on her bringing condoms just in case. Brenda thought, *If we slept together, I would be OK; Chicago is a pretty big place, so the chances of us bumping into one another are slim. He probably didn't even live in Chicago.*

Before Brenda could respond, he was already asking her another question.

"What brings you to Italy?"

"I am on vacation," she said, "and I have always wanted to travel to Italy."

Even though Brenda was disappointed that he had skipped over the pleasure idea, that didn't mean they had to stop talking. It was a long flight, and she liked having conversations with him.

Just as Brenda was about to ask him about his job, the flight attendant stopped by and asked if they wanted any beverages or food items.

Marcus just said, "Water," and Brenda could see the disappointment in the flight attendant's eyes that Marcus didn't even glance her way when he spoke to her. You could tell she wanted a little of attention from Marcus, too.

"Brenda, would you like anything?" Marcus asked.

"Water is all," Brenda replied. The flight attendant sat their beverages down and moved on.

"So where were we?" Marcus asked.

"I was asking you about your job."

"I own a security company with my twin brother and cousin."

"Wait, you have a twin brother?"

Marcus chucked a little bit. "Yes, I do. We are identical, too."

Marcus chuckled a little; it always amazed people that he was a twin. He didn't understand why, but he guessed that twins were still unique to people.

"It was great having a twin growing up, but we did get into a lot of trouble. We gave our mom a run for her money growing up. I remember one time when we were eight. CJ and I decided to take paint and go into our room and put it all over our clothes. We figured if we didn't have any clothes to wear, we wouldn't have to go to school for a couple of days."

Marcus chuckled. "We were definitely wrong; my mom

washed everything, and everything appeared to be back to normal. We did get a whooping, and our toys were taken away for a good month, though. May her soul rest in peace."

Brenda said, "I was an only child, and it would have been nice to talk to someone else in the house. If you don't mind me asking, what happened to your mom, Marcus?"

Marcus could hear the pain in Brenda's voice from being an only child, she had a look of sadness on her face even though he already knew everything there was to know about Brenda.

"My mom passed away from breast cancer three years ago," said Marcus. Marcus didn't know why he told her all of that, but he changed the subject from him to her by asking, "Now what do you do, Brenda?"

Brenda could tell that Marcus didn't want to talk about his mother. So she answered the question to change the subject. "I am a writer; I love writing romance novels. I like to keep it short, but I just love bringing the characters to life. It's something about happy endings that makes me want to keep writing."

Marcus could listen to her talk all day; she had the softest voice ever, and it just caressed him in many ways.

"What do you do in your free time, Brenda?"

The way he said her name lit her whole body on fire. It woke every inch of her body up. Even the parts that hadn't been touched by a man in a very long time.

"Free time?" Brenda said. "I really don't have free time

besides me being on this vacation. You could say I am a workaholic."

"So let me get this straight. You write romance novels. That must be very entertaining. Does that mean that you have someone waiting for you back home?"

Marcus knew that she didn't have anyone back home, but she didn't know that he knew. He wanted to see if she would shy away and lie.

Brenda didn't know what to say; she felt her mouth go dry as she tried to swallow. He was being blunt with her right now. "No, I do not, Marcus."

That is exactly what Marcus wanted to hear. He knew he shouldn't be crossing the line the way he was about to, but with Brenda, he was a different person. He felt that he could talk to her about anything and not be judged. He felt connected to her.

"I want to offer you a proposal," Marcus said.

Brenda cocked her head to the side and looked at Marcus. She had a feeling what it would be about, but she wasn't 100 percent sure.

"What proposal would that be, Marcus?"

"I have never done or said this before to a woman, promise. I'm just going to say it. I am attracted to you, Brenda, and I want to do things to your body like I have never done to another woman."

Brenda couldn't believe the words coming out of his mouth. She was excited and nervous all at once. Could this be happening to her? Could this be true? Brenda wanted the same thing, from the moment their eyes had connected in the airport to the moment he had started undressing her with his eyes.

She couldn't even speak. She just nodded her head yes.

"Follow me into the bathroom, Brenda. I want to do things to your body that cannot wait until we land. If you are interested, meet me in the bathroom in two minutes. If not, I will understand."

Marcus got up and walked away.

Brenda didn't know what to do. Did she want to have sex on a plane in a bathroom with a stranger? And would it be sex? It could just be a make-out session. Mmm, maybe she should; she was on vacation, and she could at least get new romance scenes for her books.

Sometimes it was hard for Brenda to write romance and not have actual sex. Most of her scenes came from her own fantasies that she wanted to happen in her life, and she hoped that one day she would be able to live them out. Maybe today was that day.

Her mind was saying no, but her legs, well, that was a different story. What the hell? Brenda got up and walked to the bathroom. She got to the door and put her hand on the knob.

What in the world am I doing? she thought. But before she could think any further, she was pulled into the bathroom by Marcus.

"I won't kiss you just for the sake of time," he said. "I want this to be interesting. A new level for the both of us. Two strangers on a plane having sex."

Marcus had never had sex on a plane before, either, so this was new and exciting for him, too.

Brenda was excited; she was extremely wet and waiting for Marcus to enter her. She didn't know exactly how he would do it, but she was ready, with no regrets.

"Here, bite down on this." Marcus gave her a towel. Brenda gave him a look of "what for?"

"It's to muffle your screams. I don't know if you are a screamer. Turn around, and put your hands on the sink."

Brenda took the towel, and she put her hands on the sink as Marcus pulled her pants and thong down. She was glad that she was wearing her new matching set, because otherwise he would have been pulling down her granny panties.

"Are you ready, Brenda?"

Brenda was as ready as she ever was going to be; she was about to have sex on a plane in a bathroom with plenty of witnesses. She couldn't help but smile; her best friend would be so proud of her. Brenda opened her mouth and said, "Yes."

And at that moment, Marcus plunged into her, and she heard a growl come from the back of his throat. He began to move in and out of her very slowly, giving her time to adjust to his size. Brenda knew that she was extremely tight, but she didn't care; this felt amazing. She was excited to be doing something out of her comfort zone. Jacki had told her she needed to get out more and live life.

Brenda felt exactly as Marcus imagined—tight and wet. Her butt was nice and firm. His hands fit perfectly around her small, slim waist. Something was happening to his heart that he couldn't quite put his finger on.

He wanted to prolong having sex with her, but he knew that they needed to get back to their seats before anyone began to wonder where they had both gone. Marcus moved Brenda's hair to her left shoulder. He bit down on her earlobe and whispered sweet things in her ear.

Marcus could hear her moaning. He released her ear and sped up. He looked down at Brenda's butt and watched as it bounced back and forth. That made him even harder, and he knew he was going to come at any moment. He could feel Brenda shaking, so he knew she was on the verge of coming, too.

He reached in front of her shirt and grabbed both of her breasts and began to massage them as he continued to pound into her. He leaned her back against his chest so that he could whisper in her ear.

"Brenda, you feel so good and tight. I don't know how much longer I can hold on. But I am coming baby, and I want you to come, too."

That was all Brenda needed to hear before she came, and she came hard. She let out a loud muffled scream since she did have the towel in her mouth. Marcus followed right behind her and came, too. They stayed connected for a minute.

Marcus pulled out, cleaned himself off and then Brenda. He said, "You head out first, and I will be right behind you."

Brenda nodded her head and immediately walked out of the bathroom. She looked around the plane to make sure that no one was looking in her direction. She walked with her head down, because she didn't know if people had heard them or not.

It wasn't that she was ashamed; she was thrilled at what had just happened. She had never come before in her life, so that was an experience to remember. She hadn't even known that she could scream that loud from having an orgasm.

Marcus slid his way back into the seat right next to hers. "How are you feeling, Brenda?"

Brenda just looked at Marcus, but before Brenda could respond, the airplane started making funny noises, and the oxygen mask dropped down.

CHAPTER THREE

BRENDA WAS STARTING to freak out. She looked to Marcus for support; she didn't know what was happening. Brenda hurried up and grabbed her oxygen mask hovering in front of her. The plane was shaking due to the turbulence, but it felt much worse to Brenda. This couldn't be happening to her; this was why she hated to fly.

Marcus looked to Brenda and knew she was terrified. Marcus was trying to figure out what the hell was going on. First, he made sure that Brenda was secured before he put on his breathing mask, even though he knew he wasn't supposed to do that. He prayed to God that the plane wouldn't crash. It would just be his luck. He grabbed Brenda's hand, reassuring her that everything was going to be OK.

Marcus heard the pilot come over the speaker saying, "We will be performing an emergency landing in Spain. We are coming in fast, so brace yourself and prepare for landing."

Brenda was so confused as to what was happening. One minute she and Marcus were in the bathroom having a little fun, and before she knew it, the plane was going down. Even though Spain was another beautiful country she wanted to visit, but not under these circumstances. Brenda saw her life flash before her eyes. Brenda was terrified of what was happening; she didn't want to die without being identified. Usually in plane crashes, it is harder to identify the bodies. She still wanted to remarry one day and have children. She wanted to grow old with someone. She felt the tears rolling down her face, and she could hear people crying behind her.

The pilot interrupted her thoughts. He came on the speaker again and said, "Hold on tight, guys; we are going in hot."

Brenda grabbed onto Marcus's hand and squeezed it. At least if they were going to die, she would die knowing she had just had incredible sex. The plane hit the runway. Both her and Marcus's head hit the top of the aircraft. The overhead luggage bin opened, and things were falling out.

The plane was bouncing up and down, so even though they had on seat belts, their bodies were bouncing right along with the plane. The wheels made some type of skidding noise before the plane came to a complete full stop. Everyone on the plane began to cheer. The ambulance and fire trucks were outside of the airplane waiting for people to exit. Brenda could see the news reporters outside. She said a tiny prayer and waited her turn to exit the plane.

Brenda was able to get herself a reservation into the nearest hotel room. She didn't know how long she would be in Spain; she just knew that she was extremely exhausted. She looked around the airport one last time for Marcus, hoping he would stay at the same hotel as her. For some reason, he made her feel comfortable and safe.

They had gotten separated when they had got off the plane due to the medics trying to make sure everyone was all right. Brenda didn't see him, so she headed out of the airport to grab a taxi. She hoped that they would see each other again.

Marcus was talking to the crew who managed the aircraft and was trying to figure out what had happened. He noticed Brenda looking around the airport; he wanted more than anything to go to her. She looked so lost and tired; he could see her eyes from across the way and saw that they were swollen from crying.

But he still needed to figure out what had happened with the plane. He knew it was no accident, and something about the whole situation just didn't sit right with him. He felt his phone vibrating in his pocket. He looked at the caller ID and saw that it was his twin brother, CJ, calling.

CJ said, "You good? I saw on the news that your plane had a little malfunction and you guys had to do an emergency landing in Spain."

Marcus wasn't surprised that his brother had found out what had happened; he was always staying on top of the news.

Marcus replied, "I'm good. I'm trying to figure it out

myself. But do me a favor; find out what hotel Brenda is staying in and book a room right next to hers for me."

"What am I, your personal assistant? It sounds to me like you have some feelings for this Brenda."

He heard CJ chuckle. "Mind your own business, and do it for me. I did almost just crash."

"Yeah, yeah, call when you have more information. Stay safe."

Just as Marcus was finishing up at the airport, his phone buzzed from an incoming text. CJ had come through with Brenda's information; she was staying at the Marriott just a few miles away from the airport.

As Marcus got inside the taxi, he thought about what the mechanic had told him. Basically someone had deliberately cut the fuel to the left wing of the plane, which caused the malfunction. Marcus had found out that it was also meant to look like an accident. So whoever did it knew what he or she was doing or hired someone to do it.

Marcus wouldn't get the full report until tomorrow morning, and that's when he would call CJ with the update to let him know what was going on. He decided he needed answers from Kennedy. It was becoming too complicated. Kennedy picked up on the second ring.

"Marcus is everything all right?" Kennedy asked.

"No, it is not, Kennedy. I need answers about Brenda. Someone just tried to deliberately crash the plane, so I need to know what kind of trouble she is in. I know bits and pieces from my own research, but how deep does this go? Whoever is willing to take down a plane with dozens of other people has a lot of balls."

Kennedy said, "Brenda is my biological daughter. I didn't find out about her until I was reading the newspaper one day and saw a picture of her mother in the obituary section and it mentioned she was in a car accident. It had a statement from her daughter in there. I got a hold of the police report and found out that her daughter had collected the body. I hired some people to get a hold of Brenda's DNA to test it against my own. The test came back positive. Brenda is a match to me, making her my daughter.

"All I know, Marcus, is that it has to do with her ex-husband, and he dragged Brenda into this whole situation. They won't stop until they get what they want. I believe they want her ex-husband. I offered them money, but I think it's more than just money."

"I thought her husband was dead?"

"Me, too, but the people after him think otherwise."

Marcus couldn't believe his ears. Brenda was Kennedy's daughter, and now she was mixed up in some mess because of her ex-husband.

"OK, thanks for that information, Kennedy. I will keep you posted."

They hung up.

As the cab pulled up to the hotel, Marcus wondered if Brenda was still up. He was shocked about the information

Kennedy had just shared with him. How could anyone do half the things Brenda's ex-husband was doing even when they were dead? Marcus still couldn't shake his feelings for her; there was just something about Brenda that he wanted to protect.

Marcus paid the cab driver and got out; all he had to do was get his room key, because his room was already paid for, thanks to his brother. As he got off the elevator and headed toward his room, he saw Brenda's door and heard a noise coming from the television. He kept walking because maybe she was that person who slept with the television on.

Then he heard a thud, so he retraced his steps and knocked on the door. Brenda opened the door, and there she stood, wearing a black-silk, lingerie robe that was see-through. He could see her black-lace bra and panties, which came up to midthigh and hugged every curve on her body. His mind went back to them in the airplane bathroom. Her hair was now pulled up into a messy bun. Marcus was taken back; she looked like a goddess.

"Hey, Marcus, would you like to come in?"

CHAPTER FOUR

MARCUS ENTERED BRENDA'S room. She hurried up and grabbed her hotel robe. Marcus wished she wouldn't have done that. It's not as if he hadn't seen her before. Maybe it was a security issue.

"Brenda, how are you holding up?"

"I'm fine."

Marcus looked down at her hands and saw that they were shaking. He grabbed her hands because he knew she wasn't fine.

"Hey," he said, "everything will be OK, I promise."

"I don't know about that, Marcus. One minute we are having a good time, and then the next…" Her words faded off. "Now we are in a hotel in Spain, wondering what the hell happened back there. Do you even know what happened?"

Marcus saw a tear drop down from Brenda's eye, and he knew that she was shaken up about the whole situation. He knew that now was not the right time to tell her. He moved in closer, put his hand under her chin, and said, "You're safe now, and everything will be OK. Do you trust me?"

Even though Brenda had just met him, there was something about Marcus that she did trust. She nodded her head
yes. Marcus was looking into Brenda's eyes, and he couldn't
help but lean in and give her a kiss. He hadn't got to kiss her
luscious lips earlier, so this time around, he would cherish
them like gold.

Her lips were everything he had imagined, soft and
plump, and she was returning the kiss like she had wanted
it, too. He slipped his tongue inside her mouth. He could
taste her minty tongue from the toothpaste she probably
used. Their tongues began to do a dance as if it wasn't their
first kiss.

He heard a moan from the back of her throat. Marcus
knew he shouldn't go down this road again, but Brenda was
like a drug that he couldn't get enough of. Brenda still did
not know his true identity, so he felt a little guilty. But his
body and mind wanted to have her again. No, it needed her
again. It was like he craved her; she was the missing piece
to his puzzle.

Brenda was going crazy inside. The kiss brought sparks
to her body that she never knew she had; it felt like her
body was coming back to life. The way Marcus treated her
lips, it was gentle, as if they were making love just by using
their tongues. He was gentle but demanded more at the
same time.

Brenda wrapped her arms around his neck, and Marcus
pulled her closer so that her body fitted close to his. He was

rubbing the small area of her back in a circular motion. It was like he was massaging all of her problems away.

Marcus pulled away and asked, "Brenda, are you sure you want to continue this? I don't want it to seem like I am taking advantage of you. There are things you do not know about me, about my job, and about what I do. I can easily just walk away right now and go to my room, and we can forget that this was about to happen."

Brenda didn't want to think about that. She wanted to concentrate on the here and now. She would worry about the consequences later. She needed Marcus; he made her feel secure.

"I'm sure I want to do this, Marcus," she said.

Marcus slipped both of her robes off her body and stepped back just to admire her figure. Everything about her screamed "goddess!" Marcus stepped forward and took his hand and unsnapped her bra as he slid her panties down to her ankles.

As he stood up, he slid his hand along her body, touching every part. He stopped on her breasts. He began to knead them in his hand until he felt her nipples become rock hard. Brenda was moaning in Marcus ear, which brought his manhood alive. He wanted to take his time with Brenda.

"Beautiful, absolutely gorgeous," he said.

Brenda had never felt the way she felt right now, not even with her ex-husband. His words made her feel like she was the prettiest woman in the world. Marcus stepped forward, and Brenda stepped back. Marcus didn't understand why she had done that.

"Your turn," she whispered. "Undress yourself."

She didn't know where all her boldness was coming from, but she liked it. Marcus was staring into her eyes as he pulled his shirt over his head. He heard her gasp, and he chuckled a little bit.

Even though they'd had sex earlier, she had never turned around to face him, so she didn't even know what his body looked like. Plus all he had done was unzip his zipper on the plane. In his line of work, he had to stay fit. He kicked off his shoes and pulled his pants and boxer briefs down. And his manhood popped out.

Brenda couldn't help but stare; everything about him screamed masculine. He had a solid eight-pack; there was not one ounce of fat on his body. Her eyes dropped down to his manhood, and Brenda couldn't believe that this was about to happen for the second time.

She was excited. She walked over to Marcus and kissed him on the lips and started massaging his manhood. Marcus leaned his head back, and she heard a growl come from the back of his throat.

Marcus had to take control of the situation before he came all over the place. He grabbed her hands and pulled them behind her back. He moved his free hand down to her hidden treasure. She was extremely smooth down south, and he could tell she was nicely groomed.

He inserted his index finger inside her honey pot, and found her clit with his thumb. That's when he knew he found her magic spot because she began moaning. He stuck two more fingers inside of her slowly, just to give her time to adjust. Brenda's eyes flew open as she smiled at him. She was a little sore from earlier, but it felt good.

Marcus wanted to give her everything. No, he needed to please her like he never pleased a woman before. It was his mission—to make sure she was satisfied.

Brenda finally nodded her head and gave Marcus the OK to continue. Marcus could tell that Brenda was enjoying herself because she began rocking back and forth on his fingers, but Marcus wanted to taste her instead and have her come in his mouth.

Marcus pulled his fingers out, kissed her on the lips, walked her over to the bed, and sat her on the edge. He dropped down to his knees; he needed to taste her. He put one of her legs up on his shoulder to have easier access.

He stuck his tongue inside of her honey pot and moved it in and out and then in a circular motion. He moved his tongue over her clit. He began teasing her by going fast and then slowing down. He removed her legs from around his shoulder. He then asked her to put her hands behind her knees and hold that position. Marcus looked up at her and saw when she threw her head back. She began whispering his name repeatedly.

Brenda didn't know what was happening to her; she had

never felt the way she was feeling at this moment with any-body. Even during her marriage, her husband had refused to go down on her. He had told her that it was disgusting. She grabbed Marcus by the hair and pushed his head closer inside of her.

Her stomach began to tighten, and she knew she was on the brink of coming. Her legs began to shake like she no longer had control over her entire body. She could feel the sweat dripping down her face. Her hair clung to her skin, and next thing she knew, she was screaming Marcus's name at the top of her lungs. Once Brenda came back down to Earth, she looked at Marcus. She could tell that he wanted more, and so did she.

Marcus got up from his knees and kissed Brenda on the lips. He was rock hard. If that wasn't the sexiest thing he had ever done with a woman, then he didn't know what was. She looked so good after she came. Her eyes were glistening, and her face brightened up.

All he said was, "Would you like more?"

Brenda nodded her head yes. So he grabbed her by the hands and walked her to the bathroom.

CHAPTER FIVE

MARCUS TURNED THE shower on and made sure it was the perfect temperature. He stepped in first, still holding on to Brenda's hand as he helped her step inside. Marcus made sure that Brenda's face was toward the shower head while he stood behind her. He looked around and noticed her essentials on the shower ledges.

He poured her vanilla soap into his hand and lathered them up, and then he began massaging it all over her back in a slow, circular motion. He moved over her butt, massaging it in slow motion. He wanted to make sure that he touched every inch of Brenda's body. He massaged her legs and feet.

He stood back up, bringing Brenda's body close to him, and he began on her front. He started with her breasts. He could feel when her nipples got hard, so he moved down to please the other parts of her body, making sure he spent extra time on her honey pot.

Brenda couldn't take any more of this massage; she

needed Marcus to be inside of her. "Marcus, I need you now."

"Not yet, sweetheart."

He pulled her even closer to him to where there was no space and began kissing her neck. Brenda started moaning, and she could feel her temperature rising due to the excitement. Even though the water temperature felt ice cold against her skin on the inside she was on fire. Marcus was teasing her in every way possible.

He was hitting all her main spots at once. Marcus was playing with her honey pot, massaging her breasts while kissing her neck softly. Her knees felt weak. If it wasn't for Marcus being behind her, she probably would fall.

Since Marcus didn't want to play fair, she would play his little game, too. She reached behind her and grabbed his manhood. Maybe doing this would speed up the process. He began whispering her name in her ear, which only turned her on more.

"Now," Marcus said as he turned her around and pushed her back against the bathtub tile.

She faced him, and he could only look into her eyes. He lifted her up, and she wrapped her legs around his muscular waist. He kissed her lips as he entered her at a slow pace. Her head fell onto his left shoulder; he made sure she adjusted before he began to move. Their bodies moved in sync as if they had been making love all their lives. Marcus began biting her neck. Brenda dug her nails into his back and began sliding her fingernails up and down.

Marcus had never felt this way before. Being inside of Brenda felt so right. He felt his control slowly slipping away; he never wanted it to end.

Marcus wanted to get deeper inside of her but from a different angle, so he unwrapped her legs from around his waist. He put his arm under her right knee so that her foot was almost touching his shoulders, while one foot stayed planted on the ground. He looked Brenda in the eyes, and he began going faster.

Brenda's screams were getting louder. He didn't want it to end, not just yet, so he slowed down and began the slow pace again, moving his body in circular motions. When he knew her body had calmed down, he would speed up again. He let go of her leg, took her hands from around his neck, and put them above her head.

"Brenda, wrap your legs around my waist again, but this time around, you get to do all the moving."

Brenda did what she was told. It felt different with her being in control. He grabbed one of her breasts and squeezed it. He then put her breast in his mouth and began sucking and biting it with his gorgeous mouth. Her nipples became tighter as he did this, and he knew she was about to come.

Brenda was going crazy; she couldn't hold on much longer. Brenda was so excited that Marcus was a great multitasker. She heard Marcus speaking to her.

"Brenda, I can't hold it anymore. I need to come, and I want you to come with me. Come for me, Brenda."

That's when it happened; she came hard, and he followed right behind her.

Marcus didn't know what had happened; he felt as if Brenda was the missing piece from his life. He had just met her, but there was something about Brenda that made his heart do a little dance. Marcus had zoned out for a little bit, so he hadn't caught what Brenda had said.

"Earth to Marcus. Are you OK?"

He looked at Brenda and saw something in her eyes, like she needed reassurance that what they had done was not a mistake. He kissed her on the lips, reassuring her that he didn't regret a thing.

"Yeah, I am good; how do you feel?"

"I feel amazing and tired; I don't think I have ever had sex the way we just did."

"Well, that's good to hear, and Brenda, I don't regret anything that just took place here. I just want you to know that."

Brenda just looked at Marcus and smiled. He could tell that she was relieved by the words she had just heard, which was strange; he would make sure to ask her about it later.

Marcus said, "Let's get out of here. The water is starting to get cold, and we are slowly turning into prunes."

Marcus grabbed the towel that was in the bathroom and began drying himself off. He turned around and picked

Brenda up out of the shower and dried her off, too. They walked back to the bed and climbed in. Brenda snuggled up to Marcus.

He looked at the time, and it read four in the morning. He heard Brenda yawning behind him, so he didn't know if now was the right time to tell Brenda who he really was and what he truly did for a living or if he should wait until they had both fully woken up later that morning.

"Marcus, tell me a bedtime story."

That was Marcus's cue to just wait until morning before he told her the truth. "What kind of story would you like to hear?"

"Mmm, tell me about your family." She yawned again.

"There isn't much to tell. It was always just me, my brother, and my cousin, Charles. The three amigos. CJ and I never got to know our father as children, considering he walked out on my mother when we were only five. But she did the best she could with raising us, and for that, I am grateful. I am actually older than CJ by two minutes."

Next thing Marcus heard was Brenda snoring a little bit. And he just chuckled to himself and lay down beside her, and they fell asleep.

CHAPTER SIX

BRENDA FELT SOMETHING against her butt and realized it was Marcus's manhood pressing up against her. She looked over and noticed that he was still sleep. She began getting ideas. She had never gone down on a man before; her ex-husband had also thought that it was gross.

She pulled the covers down and scooted down. She began massaging his manhood with her hand. She could feel him getting hard in her hand. She didn't know what she was doing, but she had watched enough adult television to know the basics.

She opened her mouth and put his manhood inside. It was warm, and she could taste a little bit of the cum making its way. She began moving her head up and down and moving her tongue in circular motion.

Marcus began to stir in his sleep. Brenda wrapped her hands around his manhood while her mouth was still at work. She began sucking harder. She took her tongue and circled it around the tip of his manhood while nibbling at the same time.

Brenda could hear Marcus moaning, and that excited her even more. She sped up the pace. Sucking, biting, nibbling, and then it happened; Marcus exploded in her mouth. Some of it was dripping down the side of her mouth, but the rest she swallowed. It didn't taste that bad. She peeked her head from under the covers and saw Marcus grinning at her.

"I thought that was a dream," Marcus said.

"No dream. You went down on me, so I wanted to return the favor. Plus I had never done that before."

Marcus couldn't believe Brenda had just done that; usually the women he dated never went down on him.

"For that to be your first time, I couldn't even tell."

Marcus took Brenda by the hand and slid her up his body. He flipped her onto her back and gave her a deep kiss. This was the most intimacy he had ever had with a woman. Brenda was full of surprises. He began rubbing her body. He positioned himself over her, grabbed a condom from off the nightstand, and inserted himself inside of her.

Brenda had never made love like this before. It was a slow pace. She could feel herself building up.

"Marcus. I am about to come."

Marcus looked deep in her eyes and said, "Come for me, baby," and began kissing her again.

Brenda's body was on fire, and she exploded, letting off a scream inside of Marcus's mouth.

"Well good morning, beautiful. How are you?" Marcus said.

"Considering everything that happened last night, that was the best sleep I have had in a while. And I am famished."

"Well, then let's order us some room service."

As Marcus did the ordering of the food, she went into the bathroom to freshen up. By the time she was done, breakfast was there, and Marcus was setting up everything on the table.

"Jeez, Marcus, this is a lot of food."

He had literally ordered every single item from the breakfast menu. There were pancakes, bacon, eggs, sausage, grits, hash browns, orange juice, coffee, and tea.

"I didn't know what you liked, Brenda, so I took the liberty of ordering one of everything."

"Thank you. This is amazing. You are a very considerate person."

"A woman like you, I believe, should be catered to and nothing less."

Brenda couldn't help but smile at Marcus as she bit into her piece of bacon.

Marcus watched as Brenda ate her food; he studied her every movement. He knew that everything was coming to an end and that she would be asking him what he wanted to tell her. He just wanted to take it all in because he didn't know how or when it would be over.

They finished breakfast and sat outside on the patio to enjoy the fresh breeze. Brenda had always wanted to have sex outside. She got out of her seat and walked over to Marcus and sat in his lap.

"You know, Marcus," she said, "I have always wanted to have sex outdoors."

Marcus chuckled. "You're killing me here, woman, but your wish is my command."

Marcus turned her around so that she faced him, and he lifted her up and slid her over his manhood.

Brenda sped up the pace; she didn't want to get caught, but the excitement kept her on edge. She got to be on top and be in control. She and Marcus came together. She kissed him on the lips and cleaned up.

Then she said, "So what did you want to talk to me about, Marcus?"

At that moment, he knew that she deserved the truth. Even if she pushed him away, he wanted her to know the truth about him, especially since he had fallen in love with her.

Marcus didn't know when it had happened, but he didn't want to lose this woman; he could see himself spending the rest of his life with her.

"Brenda," he said, "I want you to keep an open mind and remember that I have a job to do. Brenda, I know that you were previously married and that your ex-husband was murdered. Your ex-husband stole diamonds from one of the largest crime bosses in Chicago, and that's why they killed him.

"Before he disappeared, he told them that he had given the diamonds to his ex-wife. Now they know who you are, and they believe that you have them. They have already ransacked your home looking for them, but of course they came up empty.

"I was hired by your biological father, Kennedy Jackson. He is an old friend of mine. We go way back, and I owe him a favor. So I told him that I would find you and be your personal bodyguard. He is the one who found out all the information about your ex-husband.

"That incident with the plane yesterday was no accident. It was deliberately done by your ex-husband's people."

Marcus looked at Brenda and tried to get a read on her. He had just shared lots of information with her. He kept studying her face, but nothing. She just stood there and looked at him.

"Brenda?"

Brenda couldn't believe what she was hearing. Her father? Her mom had said it was a one-night stand. And Marcus knew everything there was to know about her and her ex-husband. Here she thought she was lucky by meeting a fine man at the airport. And that cheating, bastard ex of hers kept getting her into danger and trouble. If she could, she would bring him back to life and kill him again herself.

Brenda could hear Marcus calling her in the background, but her mind was overwhelmed at this point. She didn't know if she should talk to Marcus or tell him to get out. She was tired of being lied to by everyone. All she wanted was a damned vacation. Was that too much to ask?

Brenda was starting to reconsider and deciding to give him a chance. Then she heard Marcus call her again, and at this point, she could have blanked out and killed him, too.

"I think you should leave, Marcus," she said.

"Brenda, can we just talk about this? I know you are feeling a little confused right now, and I am sorry."

"'Confused' has nothing to do with my feelings. Let me ask you something, Marcus. Do you know what it's like to be lied to? Cheated on? Discover that you have a father you never knew of because your mom said it was a one-night stand, only to find out you do have a father? Have a guy you just met do things to your body that has never been done before? *No?*

"Then don't tell me I'm confused. I divorced my husband because of his lies, infidelity, and because of the way that he made me always feel, less of a woman all the time. Then you come in my life and do practically the same thing. I understand you have a job to do, but next time don't have sex with the job."

That last part hurt Marcus because he was into Brenda a lot.

Marcus had his answer to why she needed reassurance after sex, and now he felt guilty. Marcus didn't want to leave her alone because of everything going on, but he also didn't want to push her even farther over the edge. Someone was out to kill her, and he couldn't just leave her.

He loved Brenda, but the look in her eyes said that she

couldn't handle another thing on her plate. Marcus took out his business card and set it on the nightstand as he turned to get dressed. Luckily earlier he had put a bug in her cell phone while she was in the bathroom before breakfast had arrived. He would be able to track her at all times.

He walked to the door and turned the knob, but before he left, he said, "If you need anything, just call or knock on the door. I am right next door to you."

Brenda just stood there, not saying a thing. Marcus opened the door and left.

CHAPTER SEVEN

BRENDA SAT IN the middle of her bed. She refused to cry. Instead she got out of bed and began to pack. All she wanted to do was go home and forget that this whole trip had ever happened. She got dressed and completed packing some of the items she had taken out.

She took one last look around, making sure that she hadn't forgotten anything. She made sure to grab Marcus business card and headed down stairs to the lobby to grab a taxi back to the airport. Once she got back to the airport, she was able to get a flight back to Chicago.

She thought about texting Marcus and letting him know that she was headed home, but Brenda decided not to. Maybe she would text him when she landed in Chicago. Instead she decided to call Jacki.

"Brenda, where have you been its been a good three days. You told me you would call when you landed. That was Wednesday and today is Saturday. What happened girl?"

Brenda couldn't help but laugh. "I have been preoccupied."

"What is the matter sweetie you sound upset.?"

"I am on my way back home I should arrive Sunday night. I just wanted to let you know. Plus I just needed to hear your voice."

"Brenda you know that I am always here for you I will see you when you land."

"OK talk to you later Jacki." Brenda hung up the phone. As Brenda was getting ready to board her flight, she noticed a creepy kept staring at her. But, of course, she ignored it. She already had a lot on her mind.

After Marcus had let her know that the plane accident was no incident, she was skeptical about going home. But she knew she needed to be home. She couldn't be in a room next to Marcus knowing she loved him. She didn't know when it had happened, but it had. She pulled out her earbuds and phone to listen to some music as the plane took off.

Once Marcus got back to his room, he began to pack. While doing so, he called his brother and then immediately Kennedy after. He told his brother everything that had happened between him and Brenda. His brother really didn't say much, only that he hoped Marcus knew what he was doing and that he should follow his heart. CJ told Marcus that he would see him when he landed.

Then Marcus called Kennedy.

"Hello, Marcus, how is everything going. Have you found her?"

Marcus didn't know what to tell the old man, but he decided the truth was the best route to take.

"Kennedy, I screwed up. I ended up falling in love with her, and once I told her the truth about who you were and what I was really doing on that airplane, she kicked me out of her hotel room. I am sorry, Kennedy. I didn't mean to let you down."

"No, you haven't, Marcus; you went after your heart. I believe you can get her back. It's not in your blood to give up. My daughter sounds just like her mother. Very feisty, it seems that once her mind is made up, there is no changing it. She may be angry with you now, but she will come around."

Kennedy chuckled to himself.

Marcus replied, "Well, I did bug her cell phone before leaving, just in case. I will get a hold of you again when I am able to make contact with Brenda."

"OK, Marcus, talk to you later."

Kennedy knew what it was like to be in love. He had let the love of his life get away and hadn't gotten to raise his own child. He had never married after that, even though his father had tried to do an arranged marriage. He just wasn't going to have it. If Kennedy couldn't have the woman he loved, then he did not want to be with any other. He just regretted not being able to see his one and only daughter grow up.

On the way out of the hotel, Marcus stopped outside

of Brenda's room. It was quiet; there was no movement. He thought that maybe she had decided to lie down. He wanted to knock so badly but decided against it. If he had only known that she had already left.

The pilot finally made the announcement that it was safe to turn their phones back on. Brenda was happy that they had finally landed. She pulled out her phone to text Marcus, just to let him know that she had decided to go home. She grabbed her luggage and headed off of the plane.

She stepped outside the airport, where she was hit with a cold, breezy night. Just as Brenda was about to signal for a cab, that creepy guy from the airport came up beside her.

"Do exactly what I tell you. If not, I will stab you where you stand and leave you to die. We have unfinished business," he said.

CHAPTER EIGHT

BRENDA DIDN'T KNOW what to say, so she just nodded her head. All she needed to do was stay calm. She had texted Marcus already, so maybe when she didn't respond back to him, he would worry. Who was she kidding? Not with the way they had ended things. All she knew was that the man behind her probably had something to do with her plane's malfunction.

She said, "Whatever my ex-husband did, it has nothing to do with me."

"Shut up," the creepy man said.

Marcus had finally made it home. He was putting his key through the knob of his front door after a long flight. Then straight from the airport, he wanted to go into work and figure out the whole Brenda situation, especially the way they had ended things.

He put his belongings by the door and headed to the fridge for a beer. As he opened his beer, he turned his phone back on. He liked to keep it off when he was at the office; it helped him to concentrate more. As soon as it booted up, he saw the message from Brenda saying she decided to head home because she needed time and space to think.

He texted her back, asking if she had made it home safely. He had wanted her to stay in Spain where she would be somewhat safe. He knew he shouldn't have left her.

Ten minutes went by, and nothing. When thirty minutes passed and there was no response, he tried calling her, and it went straight to voice mail. So he called Gary.

Gary answered the phone on the first ring. "What can I help you with, boss?"

"I need you to track Brenda's phone and let me know her location."

Marcus could hear Gary tapping away at his keyboard. He remembered when he had first met Gary; he was hacking into government data trying to make an income on the black market.

All Gary had wanted to do was feed himself since he couldn't get a decent job, considering he was only sixteen. He had run away from his foster home because he was being abused, and he had thought he had a better chance out on the streets.

Marcus had actually been hired by a client to track Gary down, because he had stolen classified military data and if the information was sold on the black market, the data had the power to put their country at risk. But once Marcus had found out that Gary was only a child, he had protected him and had taken Gary under his wing because he knew what it was like to get into trouble.

"Hey you still there, Marcus?"

"Yeah, man, you got something for me?"

"I pinged her cell phone at the airport I'm tapping into the airport camera now. OK, I got her; it looks like she grabbed her luggage, and as soon as she was outside, she was approached by a man holding something against her back.

"Then they walked into the airport parking garage, and I lost them. Her phone signal just went down. He must have tossed it, but I did manage to get a photo of the license-plate number. I'm going to run it through the data base to see if we get a hit."

" I'm on my way back in."

CHAPTER NINE

GARY WAS TAPPING away when Marcus walked in. Right behind him were CJ and Charles. "You have any luck locating Brenda? Marcus asked CJ.

"No, not yet. Gary is working on it as we speak."

"Hey, guys, we have a problem." Gary said.

"What is it, Gary?"

"I ran photo recognition, and you won't believe who it is. It's her ex-husband, Malcolm, back from the dead. At least I think its him. This man here looks thin and unclean. But the computer never lies."

Everyone was speechless except for Marcus, who said, "Think about it; he could fake his own death and live free and blame everything on Brenda. But the million-dollar question is, why come back?"

"We have to find her fast. No telling what he has up his sleeve." Marcus said.

When everybody separated, CJ came up to his brother and said, "We will find her."

"I hope we do. I am in love with her. I knew I shouldn't have left her in that hotel room alone that night. I thought she would be safer there."

"You know you can't blame yourself, man," CJ said.

Marcus just sighed; he was into his own feelings at the moment.

"Well, let's go and find your woman," said CJ.

Brenda was forced inside a black van, where her hands and feet were tied up. Once the kidnapper was done making sure she was secured, he said, "All you had to do, Brenda, was stay married, and none of this would be happening." Deep down Malcolm felt bad for all the pain he had taken Brenda through. But he couldn't think of that right now. He had to look out for himself. Faking his own death was the easy part, but living and being considered dead was the hard part. He was here for money and that was all he had on his mind. He had went through all the money he had when he faked his death. He gambled it all away.

Brenda was so confused in so many ways; she didn't even know this man. He started laughing because of the confused look on her face. Brenda didn't know if she should be freaking out or not, but she knew that she needed to keep her cool. That's one of the things she had learned from her kickboxing instructor.

"You don't even recognize me, do you?" the man said.

"Am I supposed to know who you are? We have never met before," Brenda replied.

The man took off his baseball cap and sunglasses. Brenda looked at the man. He looked very familiar, but it couldn't be Malcolm; he was supposed to be dead. This man was smaller in the face, and the eyes were harsher. But it was him, no doubt about it. Brenda gasped.

"You know, Brenda, it's easy to fake your own death, especially when everyone wants you dead anyway."

He had this look on his face that Brenda didn't recognize. It was a look of happiness and evil mixed together. Brenda was scared out of her mind, but she wasn't going to let him see or hear her fear.

"So what do you want from me, Malcolm?"

He hated the way she said his name with so much distaste in her mouth. He replied, "You know you don't have to say my name like that, Brenda, as if you hated me. I told you to stay married to me, and we both could be living the life."

He has really lost his damned mind, Brenda thought. She was beginning to get upset. "Malcolm, you have to be kidding me; you're blaming me as if this was my fault. You cheated on me multiple times. I find out my plane had complications, and I'm beginning to think it was you.

"Then you kidnap me from the airport and threaten my life. You bring me back to your van and tie me up, and you have the audacity to sit here and say that if we had stayed married, we wouldn't be in this mess.

"You know what, Malcolm? Fuck you! I would have

rather for my flight to have crashed than for me to have stayed married to you."

Brenda was literally shaking, she was so angry.

"Just calm down, Brenda; don't get your panties in a bunch. Now like I was saying, we should have stayed married, because I was able to move money from your accounts to pay off my debt, but when you divorced me, it became a little difficult. That is the reason I needed to fake my own death."

"If I was untied," replied Brenda, "I would murder you with my bare hands, Malcolm, and you wonder why I divorced you."

CHAPTER TEN

BRENDA WAS SPEECHLESS; she had absolutely nothing to say. Here was a man she used to be in love with, the man she had vowed to be with for the rest of her life. How could he do this to her? She wished that she could ball up and cry, but she didn't want to show any weakness with Malcolm.

"So here is the plan, Brenda," he said. "First, you're going to wire everything from your accounts to one of my offshore accounts. Then I am going to hand you over to the people who wants me dead so that I can get away with a clean slate."

"You bastard, you would give me up just to save yourself. I hate you, Malcolm, and you won't get away with this."

"Matter of fact, I will get away with it, because no one is coming for you. Why do you think I married you? You're an only child. The best part was your mom's death during the divorce. You were weak and vulnerable. No man will want you, and if he does, just know it is a lie."

Brenda fought back the tears and said, "Well, I won't do

it, Malcolm. You can do whatever you want to me, but there is no way in hell I am giving up everything I have worked for my entire life. You're a fucking coward, and when the people you stole from find you, I hope they burn you alive."

"Brenda, Brenda, Brenda. I was afraid you would say that, but I prepared for this, too, just in case. Suit yourself."

Malcolm walked over to Brenda and put tape over her mouth and covered her eyes with an old, dirty T-shirt that had been cut up. Next thing Brenda felt was a pinch from a needle in her arm, and she was out.

Marcus knew that all the people on his team were doing all that they could to find Brenda, but he was still blaming himself for leaving her alone in the first place. He just prayed that she was OK. Marcus felt his phone vibrate.

"Gary," he said, "I pray you have something for me."

"Yeah, man, I do. I got a ping on one of Brenda's credit cards, so I hacked into the bank's security camera and pulled the footage. And it was Malcolm. He must be a complete idiot to think no one is looking for her, but anyway I used the traffic cameras to follow him and see what car he was driving and where he was headed.

"He is driving a black van and heading to an abandoned warehouse somewhere in the downtown Chicago area. Hopefully Brenda is there. Good luck. I am sending the location to your cell phone now. And will send it to everyone else, too."

"Thanks so much, Gary. You're the best. I owe you big time."

"Yes, you do."

"Thanks again, Gary."

It took Marcus about twenty minutes to get there, and soon after, his brother and cousin followed.

"OK, guys," Marcus said. "I con't know what lies on the inside of that warehouse. But we stick together, and I will run point. I am calling Kennedy to let him know we might have a location on Brenda.

"Gary called the local police, and I believe they are bringing in the FBI, because once I filled them in on the situation, they wanted to bring in the big boys. They really want Malcolm, but most of all, they want his boss. We have a lot of major players in there; so, everyone, be safe."

Just as Marcus got done giving his speech, in rolled the police and the FBI. He caught them up to speed, and they were ready to go in. He just prayed that Brenda was OK. He had to remember not to get distracted.

"Let's go," Marcus said.

CHAPTER ELEVEN

WHEN BRENDA WOKE up, she didn't know where she was. She was tied down to a chair and blindfolded. She felt groggy. All she could remember was her mouth being taped, eyes blindfolded, and her arm pinched. But something was different; she was no longer in the van.

She could hear dripping water, and she could feel the coldness inside. Like it was an abandoned building. The building felt cold, and there was a funky, musty odor in the air. She could hear the little mice moving about.

It felt empty and alone; she was scared, and she didn't want to die here. She didn't feel any source of sunlight, so that meant that this place had probably been abandoned for a long time. She knew she had been moved inside of a building, but she didn't know where. She didn't know how far Malcolm would take it, but she would never give him a damned dime. She would rather die.

"Good, you're up. I have a surprise for you." Malcolm took Brenda's blindfold off.

"What did you give me, Malcolm?"

"That's not the main thing you should be worried about at the moment."

That's when Brenda noticed the guy in the corner. "Malcolm, have you lost your damned mind?"

"No, but you probably will when my friend here is done with you; you see, they call him the Sleeper, and by the time he is done with you, you will be giving me all the information to your bank accounts. Now I was able to get some money off your card because you still have the same pin code from when we were married, but I could only pull out a certain amount."

"I told you, Malcolm. I would rather die." Brenda was glad she had changed the settings on her bank account after she was divorced. She didn't change her pin, but she did put that she could only withdrawal a certain amount a day.

And that's when Brenda felt the slap across her face. It stung badly; she couldn't believe that he had just hit her. She felt a little dizzy.

"How about now, Brenda?" he said.

Brenda felt the hot tears rolling down her face, from anger that filled her body. Just when Malcolm was about to hit her again, the guy standing in the room grabbed his arm and said, "We need her alive and awake if we want information to her accounts."

"Fine, I am going for a smoke break." Malcolm picked up his things and headed outside.

As he lit his cigarette, Malcolm heard a voice say, "I see

that it is true that you are alive, Malcolm." Malcolm's cigarette fell out of his mouth; he couldn't believe it. It was Mr.
Boss, the man he owed the diamonds to. That's why Malcolm
needed Brenda, use her money in place of the diamonds that
he gambled away.

"Well, don't look so surprised, Malcolm," said the man.
"You know, you are extremely stupid. I knew when they
announced your death that you were alive; it was just a matter
of time before I found you. Especially since you took my diamonds. You know, if there is something I do not like, it's a
person who steals from me."

"Boss, how did you find me?"

"Well, you never really covered your tracks well. When I
found out that your ex-wife's plane didn't go down like I had
planned, then I became even more suspicious. That's when my
guys tried finding her at the airport, but she was already taken
by you. I looked at the tapes. You looked rough, but it could
only be you. You know, when you started working for me we
had an agreement or did you forget our agreement."

Malcolm just starred at Boss Man.

"Well, just in case you forgot, let me give you a refresher.
Since you were already married, you took out health insurance
on you and your lovely wife here, and you made me the sole
beneficiary.

"See, what you missed again is that the Sleeper actually
works for me. I hired him on my payroll for whenever I needed
a job done. He gave me your location. Look at the coincidence;

so the Sleeper is going to take out your wife while I deal with you."

Malcolm couldn't believe that he had just been played. Malcolm needed to stall him or ditch him. But he couldn't think of anything to do.

"Now where are my diamonds, Malcolm?"

Boss Man pulled out a gun. "Do you really think you can play me, Malcolm? Tsk, tsk, tsk. How about this? I will give you to the count of three."

"I promise, boss, they're inside, where my wife is tied up you can have the dimonds and my wife."

"Malcolm you have until the count of three to hand over my diamonds no more of your silly games."

Malcolm didn't know what to do but stall. He heard boss man counting.

"One. Your face looks like the face of a liar."

"If you just follow me."

"Two."

"Or if you don't trust me, send one of your guys with me."

"OK Malcolm walk."

Malcolm began walking, but he didn't know how long he could stall once inside.

"Malcolm, I knew you were lying, but I wanted your wife to see what I do to thieves, but before I pull this trigger, what happened to my diamonds? This is your last chance to redeem yourself."

Malcolm looked at Brenda with an apologetic look on his

face and then at Boss Man. Malcolm said, "I gambled them all away. I had hopes that I would get it all back, but I ran out of time."

"You were willing to sacrifice your ex-wife for your mistake. Now that is cold.

"Three."

Boss Man shot Malcolm right between the eyes. Brenda saw Malcolm's body hit the floor and watched the light go out in his eyes.

"Get this piece of shit out of my way," said the Boss Man. "Let's find a place to throw him, and we're going to search the room he was trying to get me to go to, maybe he lied before dying."

Everyone walked out the room, so it was only Brenda and the Sleeper left in the room.

The guy said, "They call me the Sleeper because once I inject you with all these needles, you won't be coming back from anything. If you don't tell me the information that I need, I will start off by sticking needles from your foot up. You will go numb and lose all feeling for good."

He crouched down and got in Brenda's face. He ran his arm up her legs, stomach, arms, and eyes. He said, "Until we finally get here." He pointed to her brain. "Then you will just be dead."

Brenda glanced at the tool bag on the ground, and then she looked at all the needles on the table and knew she was in deep water.

"Boss Man doesn't like fuckups. Even though I come when he asks, I am still an independent contractor. That man sure knows how to lose his temper. He'll probably kill you, too, if you don't give him what he wants."

In walked Boss Man. "Brenda, is it?" he said. "Anyway I don't know why you married a man like that. One thing I don't like is people who steal from me, especially when they steal something so valuable, so your husband's debt is your debt now. He stole diamonds from me."

"Ex-husband."

He slapped her, using his back hand and causing his ring to draw blood from her lip.

"I didn't ask you to speak, did I?"

There was a loud explosion.

"What the hell was that noise?" asked Boss Man. "Go check it out."

By the time Boss Man's guy walked out the door, he was shot dead in the entrance.

It was turning into a war zone, and Brenda was caught in the middle. She was just going to have to tip her chair back to dodge the incoming bullets. She knew that it would hurt, but she didn't want to get shot. So she began rocking her chair back and forth, and then she finally fell over, hitting her head on the floor.

Last thing she heard was Malcolm's voice before she blacked out.

CHAPTER TWELVE

WHEN BRENDA CAME to, she was in the hospital, and Marcus was lying next to her on one of those hospital cots. And tears came to her eyes because he had come back for her. Marcus woke up because he felt Brenda staring at him.

"Hey, what's the matter?" Marcus sat on her bed and began wiping her tears away.

"You came back for me even though we had that falling out. The fact that we didn't even know each other that long. We literally just met on the airplane a few days ago."

"Of course I came back for you, Brenda. The moment I laid eyes on you, I felt something between us. That night in Spain when you told me to leave, I didn't want to leave you alone, but I also didn't want to upset you. I knew that I loved you and wanted to be with you.

"Wait, you love me?"

"Of course I do, Brenda. Now don't interrupt; I am trying to tell you my side of the story. I put a tracking device in your phone just so that I could know where you were at all times and make sure that you were safe. I felt so bad after all that you had been through, and all I want to do for the rest of our lives is worship the ground you walk on.

"Will you do me the honors of becoming my wife, Brenda?"

Marcus dropped down on one knee.

More tears started rolling down Brenda's face, because she was extremely happy.

"Yes, Marcus, I will marry you," Brenda said.

Marcus kissed her and slipped the ring on her finger.

"Its beautiful Marcus." It was white gold princess cut diamond ring. She gave him a kiss even though her lip was swollen from being slapped. Then there was a knock on the door.

"Come in." Brenda said.

In walked Kennedy.

Marcus said, "Brenda, I would like you to meet your father, Kennedy Jackson. I will give you guys some time to catch up. I will go home and change. Will you be all right, sweetheart?"

"Yes, Marcus."

"Hello, Brenda," said Kennedy. "How are you feeling?"

Brenda just watched the man who claimed to be her father. She said to him, "How do I know you are my father? According to my mother, she and my father just had a one-night stand."

Kennedy just stared at Brenda.

Then he said, "Let me tell you the story. I was fresh out of college, and I was starting my business from the ground up. That's when I met your mom and instantly fell in love with her.

"My father, of course, did not accept her for who she was, because of the color of her skin. My father would tell me all the time that she was just after my money. I wanted to marry your mother.

"But not having my father's approval, your mother would not have it. She wanted to be in a family who loved her and not with people who sat around hating her. Even though I come from money, your mother didn't have to worry about anything, because no matter what my father said, I never used his money. I wanted to make it on my own, but in the end, it was still hard for your mother to deal with.

"So we ended our relationship. I didn't even know she had had a kid until I received a letter from her before her death. She admitted to giving birth to my child. The only thing was in that letter she never mentioned where you guys were located, only her apologizing."

Brenda continued to stare at him while Kennedy pulled a white envelope out of his coat pocket. He walked over to Brenda and handed her the letter. Brenda opened the letter, and she instantly noticed her mother's handwriting. She started reading the letter and saw that what this man was telling her was the truth. The tears began to fall from her eyes.

Brenda said, "I still think I want a DNA test just to be one hundred percent sure."

"Well, I had to be sure myself. I already had a DNA test done way before I hired Marcus to be your bodyguard."

Brenda looked at Kennedy in a way and wondered how the hell he had done that.

Kennedy could tell from Brenda's expression that she was confused.

"When I first found out about you, I wanted to know everything there was about you, so I hired a private investigator to locate you." he said. "When the PI came back with information about you. I found out what local coffee shop you liked to go to, and I sent one of my employees there. The employee ended up grabbing your empty coffee cup, and that is how I got your DNA."

Even though Brenda was a little bit weirded out, at least she still had family out there. "So do you have a wife, or do I have any siblings?"

"No, I never married after your mom. There were women who passed through, but nothing permanent."

Brenda looked into this man's eyes. They were the same hazel color as hers, and she could see the resemblance. Even though she didn't really know this man, she wanted more than anything to have a father. She was willing to accept Kennedy into her life if he was willing to try.

"Well," she said, "I would love to get to know you, too."

EPILOGUE

BRENDA SAT IN front of her computer and began typing away. She felt a kick in her belly. She was eight months pregnant. She put her hand over her belly and thought back to her wedding day.

It was a small wedding; she had wanted to get married in Spain, where it all began. She chuckled to herself. If she could, she probably would have gotten married inside of the airport where she had first noticed Marcus looking at her.

Brenda was happy. She had connected with the father she never knew. She wore a long white lace dress. Her dress had long see-through sleeves. The front had a deep V-neck, and the back had a slim bottom that fit her body perfectly. Of course, she wore flats since she had never really learned to walk in heels.

Marcus had Charles and CJ there as his witnesses, and Brenda had Jacki and, of course, her father by her side. Marcus had looked so good with his navy-blue-and-gray suit.

Then they had spent their honeymoon in Spain at the same hotel, and that's how she ended up with the baby in her belly. Both she and Marcus wanted to wait until she delivered to find out the sex, so they were still working on names.

"Hey, sweetheart, how is the writing going?" Brenda heard.

Brenda just looked at her husband; he must be bored, because he never bothered her when she was writing unless he had nothing to do.

She said, "It's going great. I felt the baby kick, so I took a break and started thinking about our wedding and honeymoon."

"Oh, really? Well, what were you thinking about exactly?"

"How we had a very interesting night, and how much I love you, Marcus, and how I am glad you came into my life."

"I love you too, Brenda."

Acknowledgments

I would like to take the time and thank my friend, coworker, beta reader, and everything else, Edna Ferrer, who will soon become Edna Ferrer Castaneda in January 2018. She has helped me so much with publishing my first book, and I couldn't be happier with the results. She has put in just as much work as me.

She has been there throughout the whole self-publishing process, and I am so thankful that she is in my life. We have to count our blessings, and she has truly been a blessing to me.

I would like to also acknowledge my brother, Joshua Foster, for being an inspiration and a motivational person. He is only seventeen years old and has accomplished so much in his life. He is my motivation for getting out of bed in the morning.

You can learn more at:
jasminebartonmoore.com
Instagram @jasminebarton_moore
Facebook @Jasmine Barton-Moore

Jasmine Barton-Moore was born and raised in San Diego, California, where she still resides. She obtained her associate's degree in English. She plans to further her education in the near future. Jasmine spends her time as a  full-time teacher and a full-time author. Needless to say, this is the first stepping stone in Jasmine's fiction career. Make sure to look out for her new book, *Hidden Secrets*, in the summer of 2018.